Guest List

a novella

JULIE C. GARDNER

Published by Velvet Morning Press

ISBN-13: 978-0692611104
ISBN-10: 069261110X

Cover design by Ellen Meyer and Vicki Lesage
Author photo by Ana Brandt Photography

Discover more from
JULIE C. GARDNER

Find out about new releases and deals
by signing up for Julie's newsletter:
https://bit.ly/runningwithpencils

(She'll even send you *Running with Pencils* for free!)

Corie

The email lurks in my inbox like a time bomb. I can practically hear a *tick tick tick* before the explosion, computer shards slicing my throat. Would the blood be trickly and thin or a hot river staining me red? I shut down the computer and teach my classes. Try not to think. Hope to forget. The next morning Kate Turlow's all-caps greet me again.

CONEJO HIGH SCHOOL 10-YEAR REUNION.

I don't open the message, but I can't bring myself to delete it either.

Wednesday. Thursday. Friday. One more month until summer vacation. After a few weeks the email is less a time bomb and more a cucumber that once was fresh but now has turned to mush. Green liquid molding in the crisper.

SAVE THE DATE DON'T MISS –

The subject line cuts off there, but I am certain it ends with "out."

Don't miss out.

Why is Kate Turlow coordinating our reunion, anyway? She graduated with Bets, not with our class. I suppose I shouldn't be surprised. Kate's friendly enough, but she's also an insinuator. She likes to have a thumb in every pie. For a split-second I'm tempted to reply, to explain that my life is full. Almost overly so. I want to tell her I'm not missing a thing. But Kate was around back then, and she would know.

This is not entirely true.

A piece of me exists in some other undisclosed location. Or maybe I'm the piece, and Scarlet is the whole. Either way, neither one of us is complete. Thanks to Tuck, I rarely dwell on this though. The empty space. Our looming absences. *Dwelling doesn't change anything,* he says, and he's right. Nevertheless. Kate's email sucks out my air. I feel the gap, and a breeze blows through me, the saddest whistle I can imagine.

It's been almost a decade since my high school graduation, back when I assumed I'd end up writing essays for *The New Yorker*—not teaching kids how to write them. At the rehearsal, our principal, Maryann Dresden, promised it would be a night we'd never forget. Of course Mrs. Dresden couldn't have known how true those words would be. Every morning when I see her on campus now, I wonder if she remembers. If she, too, thinks about that evening. If she blames me for the fallout.

I'll bet she felt sorry for me during my interview. How could you not hire Corie Harper? *It wasn't her fault.* That's what everyone swore ten years ago, what people still claim when the subject arises. But I labor hard to avoid such conversations. Because it was, you see.

It was our fault.

Tuck wants to go to the reunion anyway. He says it's time to put the past behind us, to level ourselves at the stares of others, to answer questions with an even smile. His grin always did spread quickly, creasing a dimple into his cheek. Sometimes I trace that dent with a fingertip, the first spot on his body I kissed. I've been memorizing his face ever since. I carry it inside me alongside the shadow of its cost.

As for Tuck, he is able to compartmentalize. To rationalize. Sympathize. All the *izes* come easy to my husband. It's one of the things I love most about him. Tuck is the opposite of all things Corie. The yin to my yang, the sunshine to my moon. Which is ironic (is it ironic?) if you picture his pitch-black hair and lashes like midnight. Tuck should be the sunny one. He holds the light, while I retain the dark. Yet I'm the one who is pale, a skinny thing, dull by comparison. To this day I marvel that the man chose me, that he dug deep enough to discover who I am, who I still want to become. Tuck Slater could have had anyone. He could have had Scarlet.

But he didn't know that then.

When I admit to Ma that Tuck and I have been tense these days, arguing more often, she tells me to *let it go*. My mother's a fan of conflict avoidance, and ever since we lost Dad, she worries about my marriage to avoid crying over hers.

It'll be fine, Corie. You'll see.

But the truth is, Ma doesn't know. It's not just the reunion. Tuck and I would be on edge regardless, both of us a little scared and a lot excited. It's a tricky combination. Our emotions come in waves. Sometimes on the drive to school, I feel the flutter in my stomach, and I wonder if I'm getting sick. Then it hits me: We are trying. *Trying.*

We are hoping. We are praying. Waiting.

The *ings* come easier to Tuck.

I haven't told my mother yet, although I won't be able to keep the secret much longer. I never could find the right scissors to cut her maternal ties. She'll be after me every day, leaving messages, texting when I don't call back. She's already relentless. I can only imagine how bad it'll get when she's wondering along with me. Screening her is cruel I suppose, especially since she's lonely. How hard is it to pick up the phone for my poor mother who's simply concerned and checking up on me? I'll tell you. It's hard. Monumentally hard.

Please don't hate me for it.

I know I'm lucky. To be alive. To feel loved and purposeful. I spend my days sharing words with young humans who aren't yet immune to the world's magic, and I end my nights in Tucker's arms on the couch watching *The Office* on Netflix. Yes. Corie Harper Slater is lucky. Luckyluckylucky. I never stop reminding myself. So when Bets says it again during our lunch together, when she tells me I simply need to relax, I take a deep breath and a bigger gulp of ice water.

She means well. She means well. She means well.

"You're right," I tell my sister. "I'm working on relaxing."

Bets frowns. "That's my point." She's sitting opposite me in a sticky booth at Chuck E. Cheese, one child squirming on either side of her. My niece and nephew were both accidents, or as my sister likes to label them, *surprises*. I'll give her the *one* surprise, sure. After that, the situation smacks of irresponsibility.

"*Working on it* is the problem," Bets says. "Just chill out. Let nature take its course."

Wella, who is almost six, drops her pizza crust on her mother's plate. "What's *itscourse*?" she asks.

"Great question." Bets takes a bite of Wella's crust, then talks while she chews. "Uncle Tuck and Aunt Corie need to find out the answer."

"Right," I say. "And we're trying." I smile at my sister while I consider dropping my glass of water in my lap. At least then I could escape to the bathroom. Escape to anywhere.

"Mark my words." Bets peels off a fresh slice of pepperoni and hands it to nine-year-old Campbell. "As soon as you stop trying? That's when it'll happen."

"But, Mom." Cam's eyes go wide. "You always say we should never give up."

"That's right, baby. But you're a kid. With grown-ups? It's a little different."

"I don't get it," he says.

"Just eat."

We are quiet then, and I stare at my untouched antipasto salad. Later, after the kids leave to play in the ball pit, Bets leans over the table. Her corn-silk hair, a few inches longer and a few shades darker than mine, dangles into the pizza. I don't tell her.

"Seriously. You shouldn't be so stressed out," she says. "How long has it been, anyway?"

"I don't know. Six months. Maybe eight."

"That's nothing," she says.

I nod.

But it's something.

Believe me.

It's something.

Scarlet

Scarlet Hinden pressed a spoon against the teabag, then stirred slowly with a *clink* at her cup's rim. She preferred coffee but had never admitted as much to Clara, not in the ten years they'd been friends. If Clara hadn't figured it out by now, Scarlet wasn't going to tell her. This stubbornness was a life raft. Not that Earl Grey was a storm.

Press. Stir. Clink.

Across the break room Clara poured water from a kettle into her own cup, one from a set the Broxton family brought when they moved to San Francisco from London. Clara had been four years old at the time, yet she still clung to her accent. Except when she forgot to, which was often. More than one of their coworkers had mentioned such *intermittencies* to Scarlet. But never Gavin. He was too kind. Couldn't be cutthroat if he tried. How had such a nice man become an attorney in the first place?

Clara came to the table and took a seat opposite Scarlet. "Would you prefer English breakfast?" she asked.

Scarlet smiled. "No, thanks."

"Still too hot, is it?"

"Maybe." Before bending over her cup, Scarlet brushed her ponytail over one shoulder. Today the length of mahogany was extra-tight, pulling at her scalp. It was a severe style, but looseness made her anxious. Control was the key. Anything less might spell disaster.

"It'll taste better once it's cooled," Clara said.

Scarlet nodded. Why bother arguing?

She and Clara had met as freshmen at Berkeley, where they shared a tiny dorm room. After law school they'd rented a slightly less-tiny apartment close enough to the bay for an ocean breeze. These days, when their tight schedules fit, they took tea together on the third floor at the law offices of Olson, Brickman & Steinway.

Taking tea was Clara's phrase. Did anyone else ever put it that way? Not that Scarlet could recall. But she forgave her friend the eccentricity. She forgave Clara almost everything, mostly because Clara never asked. And also, as it turned out, Scarlet was sick to death of apologies.

Clara edged her chair closer. "We haven't had a proper conversation in a week. Are you sleeping at Gav's forever now?"

Scarlet laughed. "No. Not forever."

"I'm not complaining, mind you. These days I've got loads of space at home. Still. I miss my girl."

"I miss you too."

"Glad to hear it, but we've only a minute. Go on, then."

"Go on with what?"

"Tell me everything," Clara said. "Start with the handsome Mr. Newstedt. What's the latest with loverboy?"

Scarlet tilted her head. What could she share about Gavin that the rest of Olson Brickman didn't know already? The way he looked at her with those glass-green eyes? How his carrot-stick hair felt in her fingers? That grin. Both boyish and rugged. The man was completely irresistible. Too bad Scarlet didn't want anything she couldn't bear to lose.

"Come on." Clara lifted a brow. "How is your new *roommate?*"

"Stop! He's not my roommate."

Clara scoffed. "Don't be a cow. He's trying to convince you to move in with him, isn't he?"

Scarlet looked at her hands.

"Ha! I knew it."

"Yes, Clare. You win. He asked, but I turned him down." She raised her eyes again and met Clara's gaze.

"What's that look for?"

"Nothing. It's just... I invited him to come home with me."

Clara took a slow sip of tea and set down her cup. "Home?"

"To my mother's."

"Eleanor's?" Clara studied Scarlet's face. "You're joking."

Scarlet shook her head.

"Well." Clara's dark bob was a slice below her chin. "Old Gav must be beside himself. Bully for you." For a moment they were both silent. The scent of old leather and fresh bleach hung in the air. With its granite counters and stainless steel, the break room wasn't a relaxing space. Every minute here was billable, and Olson Brickman didn't encourage relaxation.

"You think it's a bad idea," Scarlet said.

"Not necessarily." Clara's lips formed a thin line.

"But?"

"You've claimed for months it's just shagging between you two. What suddenly changed?"

"I guess I'm ready for more," Scarlet said.

"You guess?"

"Also my mother's been asking for him."

"Oh no." Clara pretended to shiver. "Poor man."

"There's also the scholarship Olson Brickman's funding. I thought he might come to the college with me to help arrange it."

"How romantic," Clara said. "I'm all aflutter."

"If you're going to tease me…"

"All right. I've stopped."

"I don't believe you."

"Wise girl." Clara leaned back and folded her arms. "So what about that big reunion of yours, then?"

Scarlet shrugged. "I guess Gavin will come with me."

"You've decided to go?"

"Why wouldn't I?"

Even as she asked the question, Scarlet knew it was unfair. So much of her past she'd kept a secret. From Clara. From Gavin. Everyone. Still the truth lay coiled inside her. Barbed wire. A cutting reminder. Some days she kept the memories buried, but other mornings fragments rushed to the surface. Tuck's stricken face. That throbbing behind her eyes. The taste of salt and Corie's jagged sobs. In all of Scarlet's recollections, Corie Harper was sobbing.

So why would Scarlet attend the ten-year reunion? Perhaps she needed to see them again. To be reminded that Tuck and Corie were real. That the three of them had happened. That her life, at one time, had been different.

"I'm surprised, that's all," Clara said. "You're somewhat of an unsocial girl, aren't you? And you don't talk about old times, old school mates. At least not to me. Come to think of it, I've never seen a single picture of you from those days."

"I'm not photogenic."

"Rubbish. You're the most gorgeous creature I've ever seen. In real life, anyway. I don't mean those airbrushed model types, either. Bloody hell, I'd kill for proper curves like yours."

Scarlet blushed. She never tired of hearing such compliments although the neediness disgusted her. She loathed this evidence of superficiality. Yet, there it was. Heat rose in her cheeks and spread along her neck.

"Beauty is subjective," Scarlet said.

Clara grinned. "False modesty doesn't suit you. In any case, I'm glad you're taking Gav. Throwing the old boy a bone." Her grin widened. "He's been slipping you his bone long enough now, hasn't he?"

At this Scarlet sucked in her lip thinking about that morning. Gavin's skin warm against her, the smell of sleep thick in his sheets. Wrapped in his arms under the weight of his duvet, Scarlet allowed herself to feel safe. But true safety was an illusion, this she knew.

"No need to play coy," Clara said. "With a man like that panting after me? Golly. I'd never get out of bed."

"Please, Clare." The familiar tightening began, a belt-cinch stealing her breath. Scarlet didn't want to need Gavin. She couldn't need him. That's when things fell apart. "Can we talk about something else?"

"Like what?" asked Clara. "The stock market?"

For a long beat they regarded each other. Clara sipped, and Scarlet stirred, trying to think about anything but Gavin.

"Speaking of money—" Scarlet ventured.

"Were we?"

"My mother asked me to bring her another check."

"Oh dear." Clara frowned. "What did she say this time?"

"Her exact words? *What good is it having a daughter who's a rich lawyer if I can't borrow a little from her?*"

"*Rich.*" Clara snorted. "Apparently she's never heard of student loans."

"Mama acts like I owe her. Like she's forgotten I always had a job and helped out at home. I got my own

full ride to Berkeley, but all I get from *her* is grief."
Frustration bubbled in her throat, and Scarlet choked on
it. "God, Clare. I can't stand the guilt."

"Don't be silly. What on Earth have you got to feel
guilty about?"

Scarlet's heart pounded. This was twice now in five
minutes she had stepped in a pile of her own words.
What was it about this trip home that had her stumbling
over things she'd long kept to herself? "I like coffee, you
know," she said.

"What are you on about?"

"Coffee. I like it better. You never ask. You always
make tea."

"Well." Clara frowned. "Bugger me."

"I'm sorry," Scarlet said. "It's just that you might
have noticed."

"You might've told me sooner."

There's a lot I haven't told you, Scarlet thought. What she
said again—softly this time—was, "I'm sorry."

"Don't be." Clara pushed back her chair and stood.
"You can't help it if you've got terrible taste."

"Clare."

"Let's get back to work then, shall we?" As Clara
walked out of the break room, Scarlet squeezed her eyes
shut. Tears were not an option. Not then.

Not ever.

Kate

Growing up I dreamed about the usual girly things. Being a ballerina. Or a horse trainer. Maybe an Olympic figure skater. But after the restaurant failed, my parents couldn't afford dance classes or riding or skating lessons. So while they screamed at each other, I holed up in my bedroom playing with the Ken and Barbie Trish gave me when she got too old. If I sang really loud, I couldn't hear them fighting. My parents—not Ken and Barbie. I chose love songs mostly. Old fashioned ones like "The Way You Look Tonight." My favorite game was pretending they were getting married. Ken and Barbie—not my parents. I'd plan out their whole wedding. I played the priest. Me, a priest.

God. Can you imagine?

Anyway, I was telling Brian about those doll weddings back when we were in therapy (almost two years ago, if you can believe), and he suggested I throw my own hat into the event-planning ring. Our therapist (Shelly Pasternack—she's fantastic!) agreed a new career might be good for me. You know. Something else to focus on besides Brian Junior. And they were both right, let me tell you. (Shelly and my husband, I mean.)

Of course, I haven't planned an actual wedding reception. Not yet. These days it's all about Bar Mitzvahs and Quinceañeras. Believe me, I had to Google the spelling on that one and even now my iPhone autocorrects it to *qui conifers*. What the heck is a *qui conifer*? Some kind of French tree?

Anyway, with Brian's emotional support and his small financial investment (for business cards and boosts to my Facebook fan page and also some ads in the *Conejo Herald*) I took the leap, and eighteen months later, more or less, I'm on my way. Thank God I have a husband who makes a good living (not in restaurants) and who knows how hard it is to work on a business and a marriage while also raising our son. Let me tell you, balancing a professional life and motherhood is *not* easy. (I had to tell Brian several times before he truly understood.) It was his idea to call my business *Events by Katherine*. He said it sounded more elegant, more suited to my brand. *My brand*. At first I was embarrassed to say it. But Brian is in advertising. So. He should know.

And I'm happy to report it's been worth all the blood, sweat and tears. (Minus the blood part, thank you very much.) Yes, my efforts are finally paying off, or at least they're breaking even. Well. Pretty close. By next year for sure.

Scoring the Conejo High reunion was my biggest coup so far, even though Brian hinted I got the job because of his connections and not because of my professional reputation. But what the heck? I'm a deserving girl. I mean *woman*. Either way. Exactly 221 people have paid to go already (the deadline is just a few weeks away, but I'll probably let latecomers sign up because that's the kind of person I am). And even if no one else RSVPs, 221 is a decent showing according to the guy at the Marriott. His name is Wes Lark, and he used to live in New York. Not the city. I think maybe Albany?

Anyway, we're booked for August twenty-ninth at six o'clock in the secondary ballroom, and Joey Farinelli swears his crew will be done with the new deck and patio by then. They better be, that's all I can say. I'm counting on cocktails and passed appetizers in the garden while the sun is setting. It'll be real classy. As for dinner, I've arranged a sit-down, which everyone knows is better than a buffet. I decided on chicken cordon bleu because the filet is too expensive, and there's also a fish option. Salmon with rice. (I'm not gonna lie. I feel sorry for vegetarians.)

Since I've been event-planning, I've learned a thing or two. I hired Dancing Shay, the best DJ in Chaparral Valley, and I got a great deal on centerpieces from *CV Flowers*. (The manager, Ruthie Jones, owes me after she messed up the balloons for Bentley Norton's Sweet Sixteen.) My sister, Trish, is going to be our photographer of course, and she's also handling the video. We'll run it during dinner, basically a montage of pictures set to a mixtape. I asked everyone to send in suggestions for songs and also their old pictures, which I forwarded to Trish.

A few of the songs make me teary-eyed and nostalgic. Especially "Forever Young," which is almost as good as "The Way You Look Tonight." But I'm not gonna lie. I was a little shocked by the pics people sent in. Some of them weren't flattering, let me tell you. It was a trip seeing the hair and makeup and all those retro ensembles we used to wear.

God. Did we really look that ridiculous? It's only been a decade.

It feels more like forever.

Of course I graduated six years before this class (I'm still thirty-three until next week—shh), but my cousin was in their grade, and a lot of their older brothers and sisters went to school with me. Plus Conejo Springs is not a huge town. It's a blip on the radar compared to LA. For better or worse, everyone here knows each other. Like me and Joey Farinelli.

I felt a little guilty when he flirted with me last week, but it wasn't my fault. I swear. Not at all. Joey's working the outdoor renovation at the Marriott as I think I already mentioned, and I happened to be on site when he was there. (That's what we call it in the business. Being *on site*). Anyway, when Wes gave me a tour of the gardens, I was wearing that turquoise blouse that's low-cut but good for *my brand,* and Joey came over to shake my hand. Now I'm not going to lie. I let him sneak a peek. I mean, it's not like Brian's been looking lately. But don't worry. I would never take Brian Junior away from his father. Bottom line, I'm too busy with *Events by Katherine* to be messing around with anyone.

And of course, there's the whole Bets thing, which makes Joey flirting with me even worse. Bets and I, we've known each other since preschool. I mean, we're friends, sure, but really not that close. She and Joey have been on-again, off-again for years. So yeah, right now they're *on again* but please. It's not as if they're married. And sure, they have two kids together. But whenever Bets picks up Campbell from a playdate with BJ (Brian hates when I call our son *BJ,* but they're not here now so) all Bets does is complain to me about Joey. I invite her in, offer her a Diet Coke. Sometimes a glass of wine. We sit at the kitchen table, and I catch her glancing around the place. She sighs and says I'm lucky. I tell her I'm *blessed,* then I refill her glass.

According to Bets, what's keeping her and Joe together is mind-blowing sex. They fight all the time, she says, but then he can't keep his hands off her. I guess conflict is *their brand.* So when Bets leaves, I sit at the table to finish my Pinot Grigio, and I imagine the two of them. The yelling and what comes after. The things they do, and how they do it. Can you blame me? I want mind-blowing sex too.

I want a man who can't keep his hands off me.

Sometimes, while I'm waiting for BJ after school, I look around at the other moms on the playground, and I wonder. Which ones are happy. Which ones resent their kids. Which ones love their husbands. Which ones hate their lives. Thank God I don't hate mine. My husband or my life. I just want a little bit more. Is that too much to ask?

As a rule, I am not a jealous person. I've got a whole lot to be grateful for. A lovely home and a successful man. Plus a son who's very intelligent. BJ's getting straight A's in third grade, which isn't a given any more. I can't imagine poor Campbell does that well. And little Wella—that's Bets' girl—she's pretty, but let me tell you, in the smarts department the jury's out. Sure, Campbell's in the gifted group with BJ, but I don't think Bets even has her kids tutored. I get it, though. Being a Harper is no walk in the park. That family's had their share of ugly, haven't they? If I was Corie Harper, I would've moved away for sure.

In fact, I was just saying to Brian I'd be shocked if Corie signs up for the reunion. She must know Scarlet's coming. I've included an updated guest list with every email. I don't know Corie and Tucker well, and I've never even met Scarlet Hinden. Not personally. So I'm only saying this based on what I've heard. But can you imagine all of them in the same room together? If I were those three, I think I'd want to forget high school. So sure, every now and then I might envy Bets the slightest bit, but I wouldn't want to be Corie.

Not for anything.

Corie

I feel her most strongly in the seconds before I'm awake. That's when I recognize each soft curve and sharp angle of my daughter, when every cell of her is as familiar to me as the freckles on my nose, as the lines on the palms of these hands. In my bones I recall squeezing her from me (without an epidural after an eight-hour labor on a sticky autumn morning at the tail-end of a record-breaking heat wave). Yes, in the realm of half-sleep as my eyes flutter open, she is real, this baby girl of my dreams. Then, just like that, she is gone.

Before I take the test, I pour myself a big glass of orange juice, like maybemaybemaybe this will be the time, and Vitamin C is a good thing anyway, isn't it? I buy calcium-fortified Tropicana although Bets says it's not worth the money. The stuff is full of sugar, she says, and offers nothing to a growing fetus. She's probably right, but it's my ritual, and I'm afraid the one month I don't do it might be *the time.*

I'm halfway through the eight-ounce serving of my (probably pointless) juice when the timer dings, and I peer at the stick through my fingers. There is no second line. Not even a trace of one in the little plastic window.

That's when I move from the bathroom to the kitchen and dribble the remaining orange juice down the drain. So much for being frugal. Saving money hasn't helped get me pregnant.

I sit at the table and wonder about all the girls who woke up today thinking they might be knocked up. And I do mean *girls*, young things like my students who've got no business having sex let alone deciding whether or not to buy the Tropicana with extra calcium. Head in my hands, I try to picture them awaiting the results of their EPT tests. Except, unlike me, most of them would be hoping (or praying or making deals with the devil in their minds) not to see a line.

But that's not how the universe works, is it?

And so they appear for some of those girls. Two pink lines to indicate they just won their imagination's worst lottery. From reading testimonials on teen-mother websites, I've learned they rarely have to wait the full three minutes. The lines show up almost instantaneously, the cells already busy multiplying like crazed mathematicians. So far my lonely eggs have remained divided from Tucker's sperm. Ours is a pathetic half-equation.

No wonder I've always hated algebra.

So these directions on the box instructing us to wait one hundred eighty seconds before checking our results are unnecessary. And torturous. We sit near our toilets, breasts full and sore, either because we're already pregnant or about to get our periods (again and again, month after month, while I remain childless forever), and time ticks on. Slow. Silent. We either are or we aren't. And nothing changes the truth of it, either way.

This girl I knew back in high school got pregnant. We weren't close friends, but we always had Spanish class together. Our last names, alphabetically, placed us near each other on seating charts. Junior year she sat behind me, and every day she whispered to me, telling secrets I didn't want to hear. Not in either language.

No, gracias.

She was a JV cheerleader, and on game days she wore big satin bows in her pigtails. I'll never forget those bows. When she leaned in, they would hang in my face. One day she confessed she'd been sleeping with her brother's roommate, an older guy who wore Drakkar Noir. Apparently he had a cool car, and he bought her beer. So they *did it*. A few times, she admitted.

When she found out she was late, she scheduled an appointment at the free clinic. She didn't even give it half a second of thought. And she refused to tell her mother. She said her mom would make her keep the baby as some sort of twisted punishment.

"Will you come with me?" she asked. "I need a ride."

"Why me?"

"Because no one else knows."

"What about your brother?"

She frowned at me then. Hard.

Her appointment was set for the following week, and every morning in between, I prayed she would have a miscarriage. But the pregnancy held, and on the day of her "procedure" I gave her a ride because I'd promised. While she went inside, I waited in the parking lot. I didn't want to be a witness. Afterward, as I dropped her off at home, she asked if I would call her later, and I said I would. But I didn't.

When I pulled away from her house, I started crying, and I couldn't stop for more than two hours. I stood in the shower under a scalding hot jet, afraid to turn off the water. I figured Ma would hear me and think I was being strangled or something equally awful.

The next month, she leaned in close during Mr. Ortega's lesson and asked if she could borrow a tampon. When she came back from the bathroom, she had this sly smile on, just like the Mona Lisa. As if she were hinting at something horrible or maybe wonderful. I couldn't tell which. That's how mysterious her smile was.

This made me wonder about Mona Lisa's secret. Had she been pregnant with Leonardo da Vinci's child? Did she want to be? Or had she found out instead that she had dodged another bullet and wouldn't need a trip to the free clinic this month after all?

As if Milan had a free clinic during the Renaissance.

As if Leonardo da Vinci was her brother's roommate with a cool car.

Damn. People are a mess.

Thousands of years of human disasters. All of us are screwed up.

We're just screwed up in different ways.

Scarlet

The sky was orange and the sun just setting when Scarlet paused for a red light. Usually she checked for traffic and sprinted across this intersection. But she needed to tighten the lace that had come loose during her run. She hated slowing down. For shoelaces. For streetlights. She preferred to bypass inconveniences. To ignore all roadblocks separating her from her goals. Goals more pressing than editing briefs. Goals more pressing than dinner dates.

Clara was not supposed to tell her, had in fact promised Gavin she wouldn't. But Scarlet was her best friend, not to mention her current roommate, and Clara felt she needed the heads-up. Scarlet had been too busy thinking last night to get very much sleep. Today every time Clara popped in to check on her, she found Scarlet cupping her chin with one hand and pressing at her forehead with the other. *Stay awake, Scar. Now. You must.*

Olson Brickman frowned on low productivity.

Scarlet tried. But each time she blinked, her eyes remained closed a second longer than they should have. At four o'clock Clara finally suggested she go home. "I'll cover for you," she said. "You need to clear your head before the big night." Scarlet had accepted. Gratefully, even. She had only two hours before Gavin would be at her door.

He would bring her roses, she figured, and he'd be wearing that hopeful smile that sometimes made her teeth grit. Saying *no* to him was almost impossible. She knew this. She'd already tried.

She pictured him now waiting for her in the kitchen while she finished getting ready. Pulling at his collar, checking his watch to be sure they wouldn't be late for their reservations. He had texted her when he discovered she'd left the office.

You all right? We still on for dinner?

I'm fine, she'd lied. *Can't wait.*

See you soon, beautiful.

At this she felt her knees grow weak, so she went straight to the closet and grabbed her Asics. Five minutes later, she was out the door.

After four hard miles she'd finally stopped to tie her shoelace. When the light turned green, she rounded the corner, and her apartment building loomed in front of her. The vines of jasmine along its side were strung with twinkling lights. Red, white and blue. A leftover tribute to the Fourth of July. Each night when it got dark, they reflected off the hoods of cars parked below. Scarlet loved these lights. She was grateful to whoever had put them up. They were colorful. Happy. Hopeful. When she allowed herself to, she harbored dreams of her own bright future. One in which she would never feel alone again.

Her pulse raced now. From the run. From her nerves. What would she say when Gavin pressed her for an answer?

She wasn't ready to move in with him.

She wasn't not ready, either.

❧

In the end, he took it like a man, her soft insistence they take things slower. Please. She wasn't quite there yet, she explained. But soon. Maybe next month.

Gavin apologized for pushing. With her he was always so careful. However, he did remind Scarlet it was she who'd prompted him to hope, at least indirectly. Their trip to her hometown was fast approaching. There he would be introduced to her life, to her past. Her invitation had been an offer of unprecedented intimacy. He'd taken the gesture to heart, believing she was ready.

Scarlet reached across the table to touch his arm. "I didn't mean—"

He lifted a hand. "Of course you didn't. My mistake."

"Don't be mad, Gavin."

"I'm not."

She sat back. "You seem to be."

Veins roped along his neck. "It's fine, Scar. I'll be fine. And as it turns out I've gotten way behind at work so I think I should skip going home with you. Try to catch up. If you don't mind."

Scarlet shook her head. Perhaps deep down, this was what she'd wanted all along. Ever since she'd invited him, threads of regret had run through her. This train she'd allowed to leave the station had been running too fast ever since. "I can handle things alone," she told him.

"Sure you can." Gavin looked at his plate, then back up at her. He smiled. "You're Scarlet Hinden."

"Thanks for understanding."

He nodded.

"I love you, Gavin."

Another smile. "I know," he said. "I know."

Renata

At four o'clock in the morning her alarm is more of an assault than a request to rise and shine, but it's the only time she can squeeze in a workout, and the reunion is a few weeks away. While she slips on her cross-trainers, Aiden mumbles from under the sheets.

"Ren?"

"Shh," she whispers. "Go back to sleep." In the shadows she hears him sigh, then he rolls across their bed.

When she gets back from the gym, he's not awake yet, and all the pillows are piled on his side. But it doesn't matter. She's up for the day. Returning to bed is not an option. In the shower hot water washes away her sweat. Her skin is still damp as she dresses. Before leaving for work, she makes a pot of coffee and props a note for Aiden against his mug:

Please walk Daisy. If you have time.

He'd been the one who wanted to adopt the dog, but she's the one who picks up after her. Renata also handles mealtimes. For both Daisy and for Aiden. It's OK, though. Aiden's in class all day, and then he's on the late shift at night. She's proud of him. She really is. It takes quite a work ethic to study for hours then drive around past midnight delivering pizzas.

Giuseppe makes Aiden put a sign on top of his truck. It plugs into the cigarette lighter, and the cord runs out the window. Pizza delivery. With a bachelor's degree. It must hurt his ego, but Aiden does it anyway.

For them.

Unfortunately, he's scheduled to work the night of the reunion, but that's OK. It is. Aiden didn't go to Conejo High, and he wouldn't know anybody there anyway. Also they'd have to buy a second roundtrip flight, and the reunion tickets cost seventy-five dollars. Renata already decided to wear her red dress and not shop for something new. These days they're on a tight budget. Aiden's last year of PT school isn't going to pay for itself.

For a while, she held out hope he might ask for the time off and offer to come with her. But men can't guess what's in their women's heads, can they? She was just setting him up for failure. She should've told him what she wanted directly. He would've come if she'd asked. She was sure of it. After all, Aiden pulls ten dollars an hour at Giuseppe's plus tips, and the suits at Men's Warehouse aren't that expensive. Then again, if he skipped work for an entire weekend, he would make nothing. So his coming to LA with her would cost them in more ways than one.

After some thought, she'd decided it was too big a sacrifice. Especially since neither of them went to Aiden's reunion. She wishes they had, though. She would've liked to show up in her red dress with her arm draped around him. To finally see what Becky Maxwell looked like in person.

They were high school sweethearts, Aiden and Becky, but they broke up during his second year at ASU when their long-distance relationship proved too much for her.

For her. Aiden said that specifically. In his yearbook Becky filled two pages with inside jokes. They were all so *inside* she can't remember a single one. Then, as her sign-off, Becky wrote this:

A, I love you always and forever. B.

The thing is, *now* is a part of *forever.*

Does Becky still think about Aiden?

Does he think about Becky?

Probably.

She gets a knot in her stomach whenever she pictures the two of them lying together on Aiden's old twin bed. More than once she's prayed Aiden's dad would sell the place so she wouldn't have to imagine his son there with Becky any more. But that's ridiculous. She knows it is. Oliver Walker isn't going to buy a different house simply because his son's new girlfriend is a little jealous.

And whether or not Aiden cared about Becky then, she knows he loves her now. He does. He tells her all the time. *What would I do without you?* When he gets home from school and finds dinner on the table, he says, "This is delicious, Ren." Then, while she's doing the dishes, he comes into the kitchen for a kiss before heading to Giuseppe's. She always leaves the porch light on, and he thanks her every night. In the end this is all she ever wanted.

For someone to say, "Thank you, Reny. Good job."

Not that she does these things for the recognition. She doesn't. Being generous brings her joy all by itself. Some take it for granted, but that's to be expected. People get busy taking care of themselves and their own complicated lives. Their own dogs. Their own dirty dishes. She rarely dwells on the negative, but every once in a while, she does fantasize about what would happen at the office if she disappeared. Cleaning out the microwave is hardly an earth-shattering contribution to the universe, but little gestures add up to big ones.

Especially when they stop forever. Would anyone else at Edmond's Escrow make a second pot of coffee? Or find a fresh roll of paper towels? Restock the stapler? Probably not.

Why would they when Renata Howe can do it?

Once she started to tell Aiden about her daydream, but she stopped because she thought she saw tears in his eyes. (Aiden is a very emotional person. That's why she didn't explain to him that in her fantasy he's not the one delivering her eulogy. He would be too distraught to write down his feelings, let alone speak to a crowd. She has lived in Tempe since college. Almost ten years now. She knows a lot of people. Everyone would come.)

By the time Aiden welled up though, she'd already covered most of it. The organ music in the sanctuary, the smell of sweet perfume from all the wreaths. First Lutheran would be filled with flowers. Roses and tulips and lilies. (Does Aiden know lilies are her favorite? She really should remind him.)

From the casket a long line would stretch of solemn people gathered to pay respects. In her imaginings the entire space is packed. But as she gazes out over the crowd, she cannot see Aiden's face. Instead, in the front pew, she pictures Scarlet Hinden. God she looks beautiful. Brave and stoic. Just like she was in high school.

What Renata wouldn't give to be that strong now.

No, she loses sleep worrying what everybody thinks of her. While Aiden snores on his pillow, she replays conversations from the day praying she came off as breezy or charming, that her words hit the right notes. And forget about texts. Someone might misinterpret her tone. People might not get her jokes.

They might not like her.

By now she has lost track of how many Instagram pictures and Facebook posts she's deleted, mortified by the lackluster response. *Only seven likes? What is that? Meredith Twill gets hundreds, and she's not even pretty.* When these thoughts come, she feels small and mean. This is not the person she wants to be. Every morning while she's on the treadmill she promises to stop. No more comparing herself to others. She won't look up her likes or hold them up against anyone else's. Not ever again.

But then on the way in to work, she catches the light at El Dorado, and while she's waiting, it happens. From the cup holder her cell phone calls her:

Reny.

Check on me.

One little peek.

Her fingers tap the steering wheel. Maybe just once to see how many people liked her post. A selfie in her workout clothes.

Getting ready for the big reunion! Ten years. Where have you gone?

Two likes. She refreshes the page because that can't be right.

It's right.

Two people.

The light turns green, and she pulls away. The phone mocks her in its cup holder. Then in her purse. In her desk at work. And for the rest of the afternoon, she feels trapped beneath her thoughts. It's dark in there.

It is.

Corie

My entire life, I've hated telephones. Both landlines and cellular. I've always been afraid of talking on them so Ma used to make me call for restaurant reservations or to ask how late a shop was open. It would've been easier if she or my dad had simply placed the call themselves, but they knew I needed practice; that communication via telephone was a life skill I'd entered this world lacking.

On the phone you have to think on your feet, whereas with writing, you get to plan what you want to say, carefully on your own time. In a text or a letter or an email, I can work at my words, shift each one, make them bend to my will. I win battles this way, with myself and others. I don't like being ambushed.

Nevertheless.

I'm bent over my desk with a dust rag and a bottle of Windex when the knock knock knock comes at my door. Before I can ask, "Who is it?" Renata Howe pokes her head into my classroom.

"Reny. Wow." I set down the Windex, and a lump rises in my throat.

"*Hola*, Corie," she chirps. Her lips stretch wide.

"It's been a long time," I say. *A decade*, I think.

"I can't believe you're teaching in Señor Ortega's old room." Her tongue rolls the Rs, and her white teeth click. "So. *Cómo estás?*"

"*Muy bien.*" I take a breath.

"I'm not interrupting, am I?"

"No," I tell her. "Just cleaning up after a long, dirty summer. Getting ready for the new school year."

Reny peers at the posters in the entryway. *Hamlet. The Inferno.* "I love what you've done with the place."

I nod. "Come in. Have a seat."

She moves toward me, craning her neck. It's too dark in the room. When I arrived this morning, I left off three of the four sets of fluorescent lights. Not because I was trying to save the environment; I just didn't want anyone to know I was on campus. Reny takes a seat in one of the two plastic chairs opposite my desk. Her pigtails are gone, and her hair is smooth. She keeps it pasted behind her ears now. She looks pretty. And uncomfortable.

"I flew in from Arizona yesterday," she tells me. "For the reunion."

I nod again.

"Thought I'd stop by CHS today to say 'hi' to some of the old teachers, but hardly anyone is here. Guess they're still in denial about starting soon?"

"I guess."

"I did see Mrs. Dresden, though. I can't believe she hasn't retired."

"No. Not yet."

Reny pauses, but I say nothing more. "Now that I'm in town," she continues, "I'm relieved I'm not in charge of this whole reunion thing. Usually they ask the class vice president, but I guess they hired someone local this year."

"Kate Turlow."

"Right." Reny's mouth curls at one edge. "She graduated before us, didn't she? I think her cousin was in our class. Zach something or other. I might've dated him."

I nod one more time, a puppet with a single move.

"I guess Kate's a professional party planner, which, as I said before, is good. It frees me up to enjoy the weekend, you know?"

"Sure," I say. Then I add, "It's nice to see you," because that's what people say. Reny raises her chin, and her eyes catch light from the window. She looks as if she might burst into tears.

"You never liked me much," she says.

"What are you talking about?"

"Corie. Come on."

"Well," I say, before I can think of a better response. "No one likes anyone in high school." I try to smile, but then I realize it might be the truest thing I could have said.

Reny coughs. Or is it a choke?

"You and Scarlet liked each other plenty," she says. "The two of you were so tight there wasn't room for anyone else." Reny looks at her hands. "I sure tried though."

I look at her hands too, recalling the time she asked us to sign up for her club. She passed Scarlet a clipboard and loaned her a pen so she could write down both our numbers. "I'll call you about meetings," Reny said. Then she moved down the row of lockers toward another group of students.

"I don't think I want to be in Reny's Spirit Club," I said.

Scarlet raised a brow. "Relax. The digits were fake. Reny doesn't want us. She just wants to sign up the most members."

I didn't bother to argue. These were reins I happily surrendered. Scarlet was the one who decided whom we let in and whom we didn't. *The soul selects her own society,* and the valves of Scarlet's attention closed like stone. Not that I blamed her. She had reasons to be guarded. I remembered. I was there before.

The rest of the school didn't care about her then. At best other kids ignored her, and the worst ones called her names. Then, over one long summer, Scarlet Hinden reinvented herself. She lost weight and found her curves. She arrived at Conejo High a whole different person.

Who is that? the boys all asked. Even some of the seniors.

It's Scarlet Hinden.

The Hindenberg? No way.

Hell yeah it is. And I call dibs.

In a sea of familiar faces, Scarlet's was fresh and exciting. At last she had the upper hand, but in the wake of this attention, she trusted no one. Except me. The one who loved her first. So I allowed her to insulate us, to keep our friendship special. Separate. Until she let Tuck Slater in, and their easy, instant closeness gutted me.

"Huh," Reny says. "You really had no idea?"

I shook my head.

"I wanted to be friends with you so bad," she says. "I even pretended to be pregnant."

I shake my head. "But you were," I say. "I was there. I drove you to the clinic." Reny's laugh is small and sad.

"You stayed in the parking lot," she says. "I made sure of it. I thought maybe you'd pay attention to me after. But no such luck."

Heat flames my cheeks, and I am grateful the lighting is dim. "I'm sorry," I tell her.

"That's OK," she says. "It was wrong of me. Pretending to be pregnant."

"Yes," I whisper. "It was."

Reny straightens in her seat. "Anyway," she says, like the word is an eraser wiping a whiteboard clean. "I read the updated guest list from Kate's last email. You're going to the reunion?"

"Mmm hmm."

"You and Tuck?"

I nod. *Yes, Tuck and I are going.*

In the end, I'd given in to him. I've always had a hard time telling Tuck no. So tomorrow night I will walk through the doors of the Marriott holding his hand, holding my own head high. And when I catch people glancing our way, I'll pretend I don't care what they're thinking. If they've been whispering about us. And hey. At least we'll be a united front.

Tuck and me against the world.

Again.

"Well." Renata lowers her voice now, although we're the only two people in the room. "I guess Scarlet's going too."

Another nod from me. Another stomach plummet.

"What's that going to be like?"

"Hard," I tell her. "Impossible." Reny blows air through her teeth. "The truth is," I say, "I'm terrified." I drop my eyes, stunned by my own admission, stunned that telling someone feels this good. Bets and Ma have listened, but they don't hear me. Reny, on the other hand, is riveted.

"That's awful," she says.

"It is." I look up again. *It is.*

Reny clears her throat. "Don't hate me, but I'm kind of excited for the reunion."

"I don't hate you. I'm happy for you," I say. "I hope you have a great time."

She tilts her head. "But…"

I cast my gaze around the classroom. How can I explain it? "After Labor Day," I tell Reny, "this space will be full of students again. More than a hundred of them. They'll be funny. And smart. Some will be really sweet. But when no one's looking, most of them are pretty selfish."

"You think so?"

I shrug. "It's human nature, isn't it? We pretend to care, but underneath it all we're just looking out for *número uno*." I throw in the Spanish for old time's sake. I want to sound less serious. Less afraid.

"I don't know," she says. "Maybe it'll be fun?" Reny asks this like a question, still clinging to hope.

"Or it might be three hours of sipping wine and faking it for the low, low price of seventy-five dollars a chicken breast."

"I picked the salmon," she says. "And I do care about other people."

I smile at her. "I believe you."

Reny opens her mouth, then shuts it again.

"What?" My voice is soft. I almost can't hear myself.

"Can I ask you something?"

I nod one last time.

"If you're so dead set against this reunion, why are you even going?"

"Because," I tell her. "Tuck wants to. And I love my husband more."

Scarlet

She liked feeling important. Powerful and worthy. She wanted to be chosen, and she wanted to do the choosing. It was her weakness and her strength. But this need for control came with a side dish of self-loathing. God, she was tired of feeling like this.

Scarlet hated hating herself.

So she let herself be vulnerable on the first afternoon back. She was on her way to the administration building at Conejo Community College. The sky was cloudless and bright. The smell of fresh-cut grass filled the air. As she crossed the main quad, she spotted him. "Mr. Roosevelt?"

He paused. "Yes."

"It's Scarlet. Scarlet Hinden."

"Scarlet? Hey! Of course."

He'd been her AP English teacher, an earnest, lovely man upon whom Scarlet had once harbored an enormous crush. Mr. Roosevelt was the only teacher who could pull off a tweed jacket with patches at the elbows without looking ridiculous. Only a few years older than his students, he'd worn his clothes ironically.

With a wink and a nod.

Mr. Roosevelt stood before her now, tall and broad, running a hand over his clean-shaven scalp. The skin there was smooth and dark. Like coffee without cream.

"You look wonderful," he told her.

"You do, too, Mr. Roosevelt."

"Call me Rick."

"If you insist."

He smiled at her. "I do."

At his suggestion they moved to a small outdoor café across campus. Once there, Scarlet listened to his story for the better part of an hour. Several years ago he'd left CHS to attend law school but had found the career switch *unsatisfactory*. He was now back teaching English, this time at the college level.

As he spoke, Scarlet peered at him in that way of hers, the one that suggested he was the most important person in the world. After a while, she noticed a sheen of sweat above his ears. She was having an effect on him. This knowledge warmed her too. She couldn't help how she responded to his attention.

Could she?

When it was her turn, she told him why she was on campus, about the scholarship Olson Brickman was offering.

"As I recall, you got a full ride to Berkeley," he said. Scarlet had smiled then. He remembered.

"The firm is hardly doing that," she said. "But if we can make a difference for a deserving CCC kid who wants to go to law school..." Her voice trailed off. "Not that you're a fan of law school."

"Hey. It wasn't all bad," he said. "You survived."

"Yes," she said. "I did."

He checked his watch then. "I have office hours, but I'd love to help you with the scholarship. Maybe I could cut through some red tape on your behalf?" He paused and met her gaze. "We could meet up later to talk about the logistics. Tonight?" He sounded hopeful, and Scarlet's stomach twisted.

"I'm having dinner with my mother."

"Tomorrow?"

"It's our ten-year reunion," she said. Her jaw went stiff without consent. Rick nodded then, and Scarlet wondered what he was thinking. Would he mention her graduation? What happened after?

"I remember mine," he said. "If it makes you feel any better, everyone's too focused on making their own good impressions to worry much about anyone else."

Scarlet's lip twitched. "That does make me feel better," she said. "A lot."

"Then I'm glad I ran into you. It wouldn't do for one of my favorite students to be nervous at her reunion."

"Nervousness isn't my problem."

His smile was shy. "No, I gather it's not." He pushed back his chair and stood.

She wasn't ready to say goodbye.

"On second thought," she said, "Tonight would be great."

Rick grinned at her. "Your mother won't mind?"

"I'll have dinner with her first, then I'm all yours." As she said it, she'd felt treacherous. Poor Gavin. What would he think? She loved him. She really did. But if she was going to settle down, she needed to be sure.

Completely sure.

෨∾ଡ଼

The next morning, she visited the cemetery. Not that she needed to pray or ask for forgiveness, but after a night spent reliving her past, the voices in her head returned with a vengeance. They were incessant. Loud. In her experience, the only thing that quieted them was the solitude of gravestones.

When she and Tuck Slater were young, they came here together often; him to mourn his mother, her to embrace the silence. She told herself today's meeting was accidental, but as she approached his slumped shoulders, the sweep of black hair, she knew. Deep down she'd hoped he would be here. Perhaps not consciously, but still.

If this weekend were to be about closure, Tuck had to be a part of it.

So here she was again in the presence of his grief, absorbing it, taking on his ache. From ten feet away she wanted to yell at him, tell him the absence of his long-dead mother couldn't compare. That she had lost more. She had lost him. And Corie too.

But she didn't yell.

She walked up and knelt next to him in a patch of damp grass. He looked to his side but avoided her eyes. For a long while they did not speak. They simply bowed their heads, let the sunshine warm their skulls. They were beside a thick hedge, behind a grove of gnarled oak trees. Nobody could see them. This truth was freeing to Scarlet. And terrifying.

From the corner of her eye, she caught Tuck's lips moving. Did he think she could hear him? Did he want her to? What was he saying? And where was Corie? An hour later when they finally parted ways, Scarlet wondered whether or not he would tell her.

In the end, she decided either choice was wrong.

Tuck

Corie has no idea.

She actually thinks I'm making her go to our ten-year reunion tonight. I presented my arguments, pushed until she gave in. I even left a copy of our RSVP for her to find in the printer. Banquet chicken for seventy-five bucks a pop. That's 150 dollars we won't see again. But whatever. Since the job switch, I'm making more money. I told her the extra traveling would pay off. Now I'm making good on my promise. I have plenty of vacation time saved, never took off work even when I was still in sales. So Corie's going to be extra surprised when we drive straight to the airport. And hopefully extra happy. It's been a year since we went away even for a weekend. Maybe longer. Man, we need this trip.

In my mind, I can hear her in the shower. Every four weeks, like clockwork. Running water and a bathroom door doesn't hide the sound. Damn, that shit is awful. Each time I feel worse and worse. Like less of a man. Like there's something wrong with me. With us.

Like maybe we're cursed.

I haven't admitted any of this to her, and here's hoping I never have to. Maybe this trip will be what the doctor ordered. *Let's get the job done right this time, Tuck.*

Someone's at the front door now. Corie must be home. She left hours ago with her mother to get her hair and makeup done. She thinks it's *for the reunion.* Laura is in on the surprise, but she's the only one I told. I'm not sure why. Maybe I just needed her to know how much I love her daughter. Once she heard about the surprise, she offered to take Corie to the salon to *get pretty.* That's how my mother-in-law put it:

"Let's get pretty."

As if my wife needs big hair and makeup for that. To me, she's the same beautiful girl I fell in love with. I'm just not sure Corie feels that way about herself.

Or about me, for that matter.

I'll give Laura credit, though: A day at the salon was a perfect distraction. Corie wasn't even a little bit suspicious. This morning, before they left, Laura whispered that this'll be our first time in Vegas since Corie and I eloped. I think she's still hurt we didn't invite her back then, but even she's gotta understand the timing was wrong. She was mourning George hard, and we didn't want to rub our wedding in her face.

Maybe Corie and I should've waited. But after everything, well, we felt like we had no more minutes to waste. Life seemed fragile then. More than ever. And yeah it was tough, tougher than I thought it would be, but we made the best of it. Corie and I didn't love each other less than anyone else does when they take their vows. We were just a little sadder then.

I'm hoping to change that this time.

I remember standing at the altar when she told me her dad was looking down on us, that he approved of what we were doing. That he loved me almost as much as she did. Those words made me choke up, and I'm not ashamed to say it. I hated not being able to ask George for his daughter's hand in marriage. My wife deserved that. She still does. She needs something in our relationship to feel normal. Easy. Right.

What is she doing downstairs, anyway?

There is fumbling, bumping, some whispers. More than one voice for sure. "Core?" I call out. "Is that you? Come on up!" I move to the top of the stairs.

"It's not Corie." Below me, my sister-in-law appears. Her face is white, and dark circles line her eyes.

"Bets?" Acid rises in my throat. Something is wrong with her, but what? She couldn't possibly know about this morning. Jesus. Did Bets come here to confront me? To tell her sister? It's not like I went looking for Scarlet. She came to me. It was all her. I swear.

"You're home," Bets says. *Obviously.*

"Everything OK?" I ask her.

"It will be." God, she sounds exhausted. *Guilt can be exhausting.* I take a step down, and Wella clamors into view, wraps both arms around her mother's legs.

"Uncle Tuck!" Wella crows. "Guess what?" She hops from one foot to the other. "I have my SpongeBob suitcase, and Cam does too!" Bets bends, whispers something in Wella's ear. Wella bolts away from the stairs. When Bets stands again, she seems lighter. Like the hardest part is behind her.

"What's going on?" I ask.

From the top of the stairs I can almost hear Bets swallow.

"I left Joey." Her chin drops to her chest. "Can we stay here for a while?"

Kate

For the tenth time tonight I reach down and press at my nametag. It wouldn't do for mine to fall off. Branding is very important.

Hello: My name is KATE TURLOW (of Events by Katherine)

People stare at me funny when they step up to the table, like my face is familiar, but they don't know why. I'm not sure who they're expecting. They probably assumed Renata Howe would be in charge. "Where's Renata? We want Renata!" At least that's what she told me they would all be asking in her emails. Her many, many emails.

So far, not a single person has mentioned her name, though. And if you ask me, Renata Howe should be grateful I'm doing this instead of her. Believe me, this spot is a little too breezy for my liking. Who puts a sign-in table under an air conditioning vent? I expected better temperature control from a Marriott. And of course I'm not wearing a wrap. I didn't even bring one. The thing is, I like the way my bare shoulders look in this dress. The burgundy makes a nice contrast with my skin, don't you think? First impressions mean a lot. Brian says they mean everything, and he's in advertising. Have I mentioned that?

He would throw a fit if he saw that my name tag is the only one without a digital picture on it. It's a good thing he's not here. I'd have to tell him to calm down and then explain this is not my graduating class. Of course they don't have my senior portrait. Although it's a shame they didn't ask me for one. It would have helped brand *Events by Katherine*. And I'm not gonna lie. I look better than ninety-five percent of the women lining up here. Maybe ninety-nine.

Most of them stand behind their husbands (or boyfriends or lovers or whichever poor person is in front of them) wearing this slightly glazed expression. I call it a *deer-in-the-headlights* look. Like they made a horrible mistake coming here. What they need is a quick stiff drink. Maybe two. Once the cheeks start shining and the noses turn red, then we're off to the races.

That's my dad's saying. *Off to the races.* I've never been to a horse race.

So far the most exciting part of tonight was when Lenny Walberg tried to sneak in a date he didn't pay for. OK. He might have paid for her but not the seventy-five dollars for a chicken plate. From the looks of this girl, she would've cost him a month's salary—if she were a professional escort, that is. But let's be honest. There's no way he landed someone like that without forking over cold hard cash. I went to school with Lenny's older brother Simon, and believe me, the Walbergs were no Don Juans.

Anyway, I let Lenny bring in his sex-bunny. I figured, what the hell? At least a dozen of the women who paid for their dinners won't eat a bite. I wouldn't if I were them. And there will probably be at least one salmon left over. (Poor vegetarians. Yuck.)

Sadly, the Lenny Walberg excitement happened more

than an hour ago, and the truth is now I'm getting a little bored. Almost everyone on the guest list is here, so I slip off to the bar for a Pinot Grigio. One won't get me drunk. (OK, this is my third.) When I return to the check-in table, I look at the name tags still on the black velvet cloth. I can't say I'm blown away. I never believed Corie Harper and Tuck Slater would have the nerve to show their faces. Not to mention Scarlet Hinden. To be honest, I'm relieved she didn't come. That girl would hog my spotlight.

As for Renata Howe? Well. That is a surprise. I expected her to be the first one here. In all her messages she seemed so eager. Did I mention she dated my cousin? Apparently Zach dumped her. Poor thing. (Renata, I mean—not Zach.) I hope she's not still bitter. About him. About this night. Life's too short to not make lemons out of lemonade, am I right?

If she does show up, I'll be sure to remind her party planning is hardly glamorous. It's a lot of hard work making the arrangements. Months of phone calls and emails and contracts. And now I'm shivering at this table greeting everyone on the way into the ballroom. One at a time.

Brian says I have a way of making people feel special. I, myself, am just grateful I can be here to help smooth out their catastrophes. Because that's what class reunions are. One spray-tanned, boob-jobbed catastrophe after another.

I'm not being mean. Mine was, too, for better or worse. Mostly worse. The people there were all train wrecks. Everyone fronting. Spewing small talk and dropping humblebrags. It was depressing even after I got buzzed. Brian and I lasted about two hours, then we took off to McDonald's and split a super-sized fry and one large strawberry shake. Believe me, that meal was way better than the chicken they served. Come on, Marriott.

You need to step it up.

At least I got my plate for free tonight. Plus, Brian let me buy a new lipstick to match my dress. It's Chanel. The lipstick, not the dress. And I'm not gonna lie. I look hot.

Way younger than thirty-four.

August 29, 9 p.m.

Scarlet sat on a sagging couch in her mother's living room. The dingy upholstery smelled of dust. She always felt about to sneeze. By now Mama had been asleep beside her for at least twenty minutes. *Passed out is more like it.* On the floor beside them sat her oxygen tank. Scarlet listened to her mother's snores for another minute before making the call.

When he answered, she took a long breath.

"Hey there," he said. "I wasn't expecting to hear from you. How's the reunion?"

"I didn't go," she said.

"What? Where are you?"

"At my mother's house."

From him then, a long pause. "Everything all right?"

"Not really," she said.

"Oh. I'm sorry."

"I am too."

"How can I help?"

"Ask me again," she said.

"Ask you what?"

"To move in with you."

"Whoa. Scar." Another long pause. "Really?"

"Please," she said. "Ask me again."

"OK. Will you—"

"Yes," she said. "Yes."

శాం

At LAX a Southwest jet taxied down the runway. Corie and Tuck sat near the back. As the airplane picked up speed, Corie took her husband's hand and squeezed. "Thank you," she said.

"We needed this trip."

"Yes," she said. "But that's not why I'm thanking you."

For a moment, Tuck was quiet. "Bets?"

Corie nodded first, then she sighed.

"Please don't worry about her," Tuck said. "Let's go to Vegas and forget about everything except us. For two days. That's all. Just two."

"But—"

"Stop." He put his fingers under his wife's chin. "Your sister will be fine," he said. "The kids. Your mother. They're fine."

Corie looked out the small window as the world rushed away from them.

"We'll all be fine," Tucker told his wife.

"I hope you're right," she said.

శాం

An hour away in a Hyundai rental, Renata Howe turned up the car radio. She recognized the song. Pat Benatar, maybe? Yes. Her mother played it on repeat after the divorce, but Reny never listened to the lyrics. *Don't want to leave you really, I've invested too much time to give you up that easy. To the doubts that complicate your mind.*

Above her the night was gray and starless from too

much city smog. She glanced at the dashboard clock. Nine-fifteen. Corie and Tuck would be at the Marriott by now. Everyone but Reny would be there. Corie hadn't wanted to go to the reunion, but Tucker did.

I love my husband more.

"More than he loves you?" Reny had asked.

Corie shook her head.

"Then what?"

"Just more," Corie said.

Reny still didn't understand.

Tail lights lit her way now, a ribbon of red scoring the freeway. *Whatever we deny or embrace for worse or for better, we belong. We belong. We belong together.*

When the song ended, she wished it would play on repeat, but Reny had learned from another of her mother's favorites that you can't always get what you want. She flipped off the radio. Out loud she asked herself, "Where the hell are we going?"

She listened, but no answer came.

After another hour of silence, she stopped to fill her tank. She bought a ham sandwich in the gas station mini mart and ate it in the parking lot. Returning to the highway, she headed east. And as the sky cleared and the stars came out, she decided. She would keep going, wearing out the road, until she arrived where she needed to be.

Until she found the place where she knew for sure that someone loved her more.

A Note from Julie C. Gardner

Dear Reader,

I'm thrilled you read my novella *Guest List*, the prequel to *Letters for Scarlet*. *Scarlet* begins with Corie and Scarlet already struggling in their respective relationships. With *Guest List* we glimpse the events just beforehand to further explore their hopes and fears. I also introduced a new character, Renata Howe, who will appear in the sequel to *Letters for Scarlet*. Written in short vignettes from the points of view of five separate characters, *Guest List* details the days leading up to Corie and Scarlet's ten-year high school reunion.

Who will attend? Why wouldn't they? *What is each woman afraid of?*

If you liked *Guest List*, please consider leaving a review on Amazon. Reviews help other readers discover authors they might not otherwise find. Even a few sentences saying why you enjoyed the book can make a big difference. And to those of you who've reviewed already: thank you, thank you, thank you!

I'd also like to invite you to join my mailing list to stay up to date on my latest news and special sales. When you do, you'll get a free ebook of *Running with Pencils*! You can sign up here: https://bit.ly/runningwithpencils and you'll catch my next newsletter. Until then...

All my best,
Julie

P.S. Read on for a sneak peek at *Letters for Scarlet*.

About the Author

Julie C. Gardner is a former English teacher and lapsed marathon runner who traded in the classroom for a writing nook. Now she rarely changes out of her pajamas, and is an author of Women's Fiction. She lives in Southern California with her husband, two children and three dogs.

Keep up with Julie online:

Newsletter: https://bit.ly/runningwithpencils (and get *Running with Pencils* for free)
Website: JulieCGardner.com
Facebook: Julie.C.Gardner
Twitter: @juliecgardner
Instagram: @juliecgardner

Other Titles by Julie C. Gardner

Be sure to check out Julie's other work:

Letters for Scarlet, the story of two best friends—Scarlet and Corie—whose relationship is torn by broken promises and loss.

Running with Pencils, a short story about a "midlife marathon"—twenty weeks of running and twenty weeks of writing.

Read on for a sneak peek at *Letters for Scarlet*...

Running with Pencils

A month before my fortieth birthday, under the influence of inspiration (not to mention half a pitcher of margaritas), I concocted a specific plan—one that offered an obvious starting line, a concrete ending and clearly digestible nuggets of achievement along the way. For the next five months I'd train for a race. Not just any race.

A midlife marathon.

While I convinced my forty-year-old legs they could run more than three miles at a time, I would also write a memoir chronicling tales of gladness and woe. Twenty weeks of running. Twenty weeks of writing. All I needed was a new pair of shoes, a couple of notebooks and a handful of pencils, and by springtime, I'd be ticking two big items off my bucket list: completing a marathon and a book. What could be simpler?

Get it for free! Join Julie's new release mailing list and she'll send you a free ebook of *Running with Pencils* (normally $0.99): https://bit.ly/runningwithpencils.

Letters
for
Scarlet

a novel

JULIE C. GARDNER

Corie

I've always liked my nickname and the fact that those who are close to me have an easier time of it, subtracting a syllable from more formal introductions. *Corinna* is a mouthful, but *Corie* is simple, the way things should be when people are friends. Tuck digs even deeper, calling me *Core*, a single word that can be either a noun or a verb. Both imply a goal. Something central. Intimate. Four letters that unite this pair of opposites.

He's all action and go, go, go. I'm content with stillness, the noun of our relationship. Tucker is black hair and lashes like warm silk. I'm blond curls and eyes so icy-blue my sister said I was adopted from a wolf pack. She chanted *See-Through See-Through,* and I hated being pale. So thin. Practically transparent. Then one day Tuck Slater suggested I was *translucent in a good way,* and I began to count the number of times his skin chose my skin, to memorize the way his bones fit my bones.

That was a decade ago when we attended Conejo High, before I landed a job teaching literature instead of writing it. Parking in the faculty lot was uncomfortable at first. So was using everyone's first names.

Hey, John! Not Mr. Pickett.

Good morning, Bev! It still feels strange to call Mrs. Fox by her nickname.

What remains uncomfortable now is wondering what they see when they greet me in the halls: Corinna the student, the John Keats wannabe, the one from "the terrible tragedy"; or Ms. Harper, the English teacher who scribbles in journals on her lunch breaks.

Today I've barely settled on a couch in the corner of our lounge when the new assistant principal strides toward me, skinny and fresh-faced, a bag of microwaved popcorn steaming in his hands. His cheeks shine with the hope of someone starting his career, and the sleeves of his oxford are rolled up at the wrists.

"Ms. Harper." He nods at me.

"Hello, Mr. Callaghan."

He's wearing glasses of the Clark Kent variety, and his dark hair spikes upward like a head full of licorice. "That smells good." He indicates the frozen meal in my lap. "Chicken parmesan?"

"I think so," I say. "I just grab whatever my husband puts in the freezer." I shove a forkful of mozzarella into my mouth, but after I chew and swallow, he's still studying me, eyes round and quizzical.

"Mr. Harper does the grocery shopping?" he asks.

"Slater," I say. "Mr. Slater. Harper is my maiden name."

"Ah. Progressive choice."

I shake my head. "It's less *progress* and more *I hate going to the market.* Tucker—that's my husband—he's great, but he hates to cook. So he buys the groceries, and I make the food. You could say we take on each other's bigger hate. So to speak." I inhale a chunk of chicken to stop myself from rambling, and Mr. Callaghan smiles at me.

"Sounds equitable," he says. "But I was referring to the fact that you use your maiden name."

"Oh!" I cough on the chicken chunk, and my forehead warms to the point of sweating. "No," I manage to say. "You see, Harper was the name on my credential, and then my dad died, and I decided to stay a Harper. For him. Not that he would have expected me to. I just thought it was the right thing to do. And easier too."

So much for not rambling.

Mr. Callaghan sets down his bag of popcorn and takes a seat on the opposite end of the couch. He smells like aftershave and hot butter. "I'm sorry about your father."

"It's been a while, but thanks." I picture my dad's kind face, his strong hands. I drop my chin, and my hair is a drape of white-blond curls along my neck.

"Anyway." Mr. Callaghan exhales as if he might clear the awkwardness in one gust. "I came over here for a reason." His voice is softer now but still deep. I lift my head to hear him better and catch Stella Womack and Bart Kominski grinning at me from across the room.

Great.

"I wanted to compliment you on your lesson yesterday," says Mr. Callaghan.

"I got a copy of your evaluation this morning," I tell him. "You were very generous."

"It's not easy to act natural when you're being observed. But your class? It was a pleasure."

"Thanks again, Mr. Callaghan."

"Please," he says. "Call me Henry. We've been working together for a month. I think it's time."

"Has it been only a month?" I ask. "This school year's really dragging." I paste on a smile in case he doesn't have a sense of humor. Henry nudges his glasses higher on his nose.

"I hope you don't mind if I call you Corinna," he says. Behind him Bart and Stella wave and blow kisses.

"Nope," I say. Then I set down my fork and pick up the pencil next to my journal. "But I'd better get back to writing. No rest for the weary."

"No rest for anyone on this couch." His small laugh is reassuring. Henry Callaghan likes to joke. "It should be against the law," he says. "Or at least a health code violation."

"That's funny," I tell him. *A little*, I think.

"It's true," he tells me back. "I'll leave you to your work, then.

I look up at him. "My what?"

"Work," he says again. "I see you writing in that journal every day. Concentrating. Serious. I figure it must be pretty important."

My forehead grows even warmer, and I worry I might blush. "No one ever calls my writing work. Not even Tuck."

"Then let me be the first."

"Do I have a choice?" My smile is crooked. "After all, you are the boss."

"So I am," he says. "But don't forget. It's Henry."

He pushes himself up off the couch and collects his bag of popcorn. When he stands, I notice his pants could use a decent ironing. Then, as Henry Callaghan walks across the lunchroom and out the door, I watch him go from under lowered lashes.

ॐॐ

For my afternoon classes I write these instructions on the board:

- *Read the poem at your desk.*

- *On the paper below the poem, share what you think the poet implies about IDENTITY.*

- *After five minutes, pass your poem to the left and repeat the process.*

When the bell rings, the students amble into the room in packs and take their seats.

"How much do we have to write?" they ask.

"There's no minimum or maximum," I say. "Just tell me how you feel."

"I feel tired," says Greer Larson. "I need caffeine."

"Trust your instincts," I suggest. "Trust yourself."

"What if my instincts are telling me to go to Starbucks?"

I shake my head. "You have five minutes per poem. Starting now." I check the wall clock and make a mental note of when to tell my students to stop trusting themselves and pass what they have written to the left. I'm collecting the papers from my sixth period class when I begin to feel the ache. It is dull. Familiar. Regular as the tide. A hand slides to my stomach as the kids stack their work in the wire bin next to my computer.

I tell them, "Don't forget to check out your copy of *Inferno* from the library by Friday," although it has been written on the white board for a week. As they exit the classroom, I ask Troy Solomon to shut the door behind him. A stump of a boy with ferocious acne, Troy waves at me from the hallway.

"See ya, Ms. Harper."

Another cramp tugs at me, emptying my insides without permission. I listen for the click of the door latch and fumble in my purse for a tampon and liner.

৩৯৫৩

After dinner Tuck washes dishes while I remain in the dining room with a folder of student essays. I mark them with purple ink instead of red and try to write at least one positive comment for each critique. Sometimes the writing is so bad I'm stuck with *Good choice of college-ruled paper* or *Thanks for removing the raggedy edges from the left side of the page.*

Greer Larson's character analysis of Sydney Carton seems especially awful, but the truth is, I am harboring a negative attitude like a fugitive in an attic. Since leaving school today, I've cradled it, this lump of sadness swaddled in my arms. The failure leaves room for nothing else. It's all I see now, what I look for.

Tucker enters the room so quietly I do not notice him at first. Since my sister and her children moved in with us, Tuck and I have taken to creeping around on tiptoes. But tonight the kids are with their father, and Bets won't be back from her night shift until morning. Tuck clears his throat, and I look up. He has changed out of his work clothes into gray sweatpants and my favorite of his T-shirts. The cotton is faded red, frayed by frequent washings. From ten feet away my husband smells like Tide.

"Almost done in here?" he asks.

"Never," I tell him. "Ever."

"Give 'em all As and take me to bed." He grins, and I imagine I could fit my whole thumb in his dimple.

"I wish. Didn't you bring any work home from your trip?"

"Just a suitcase." He takes the pen from me and sets it on the table. "Come on, Core. These kids won't spontaneously combust if they don't get their essays back tomorrow."

"No," I admit. "They won't." I study my empty hand and remind myself that Tuck doesn't mean to minimize my career. He values teachers and me in particular. But the way his words erase my goals—even in jest—leaves me feeling hollow. Unimportant. Less than.

Act full, Corie. You have so much already.

"I missed you this week," I tell him.

"Don't you always miss me?"

"Hmm," I say by way of agreement. He pulls out the

chair next to me, and I push my gradebook away. I can make room for him. I will.

"I forgot to ask how your evaluation went with the new guy. What's his name? Calloway?"

"Callaghan. Henry Callaghan." I picture his spiked hair and wrinkled pants, hear him calling the words in my journal *work*. "He's on the young side. Not much older than I am." My lips are dry, and they crack on a smile. Tuck shifts in his seat and appraises me.

"He any good?"

I consider the question. "I have no idea," I say.

Tucker prompts me with a tilt of his head. "Come on. What does your gut tell you?"

"Stella and Bart haven't organized a lunchtime protest against him yet. I guess that qualifies as good." Before Tuck can push any deeper, a cramp cuts through the center of me, and a grimace replaces my smile.

"Hey, hey," he says. "You all right?"

"Yep," I tell him, although I'm not.

"Headache?"

"No," I say. "Unfortunately, it's not a headache."

"Oh." Tuck studies my face for the answer he already knows. "I'm sorry, Core."

"I'm sorry too."

He stands and puts a hand on my shoulder. "Guess I'll shower and unpack."

"I'll finish up here soon," I say. "Promise." When he leaves, I stuff the essays in my book bag and grab some Advil from the lidless container above the refrigerator. Throwing away the childproof tops is a habit Tuck hasn't broken.

They're a pain in the ass, and we don't have kids.

Yet, I tell him. *Not yet.*

Filling a glass with water, I swallow three tablets. Then, once I hear the shower running, I pluck my cell phone from its charger. Almost a year has passed since I tried the number, and I enter it quickly before losing my nerve. Eleanor Hinden never answers anyway. Each time, I get her answering machine with the same old message Scarlet and I recorded more than a decade ago. I like to listen and hang up without saying a word. I'm simply being kind, making sure Scarlet's mother is all right. Still, I don't tell Tuck about the calls. He would claim they're motivated by something else entirely.

Tonight the phone rings four times, and I await our giggled greeting. Scarlet's voice with my bright laughter in the background. A bridge across ten long years. Instead, there is a hiccup followed by the robotic sounds of the default message: *No one is available to take your call; please leave your name and number at the beep, and someone will get back to you as soon as possible.*

Truth settles in the pit of me, a friendship replaced by the programmed lines of a stranger. Scarlet has finally left me.

Forever.

Find out what happens next… Pick up *Letters for Scarlet* today!

Discover more from
JULIE C. GARDNER

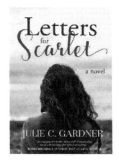  

Find out about new releases and deals
by signing up for Julie's newsletter:
https://bit.ly/runningwithpencils

(She'll even send you *Running with Pencils* for free!)